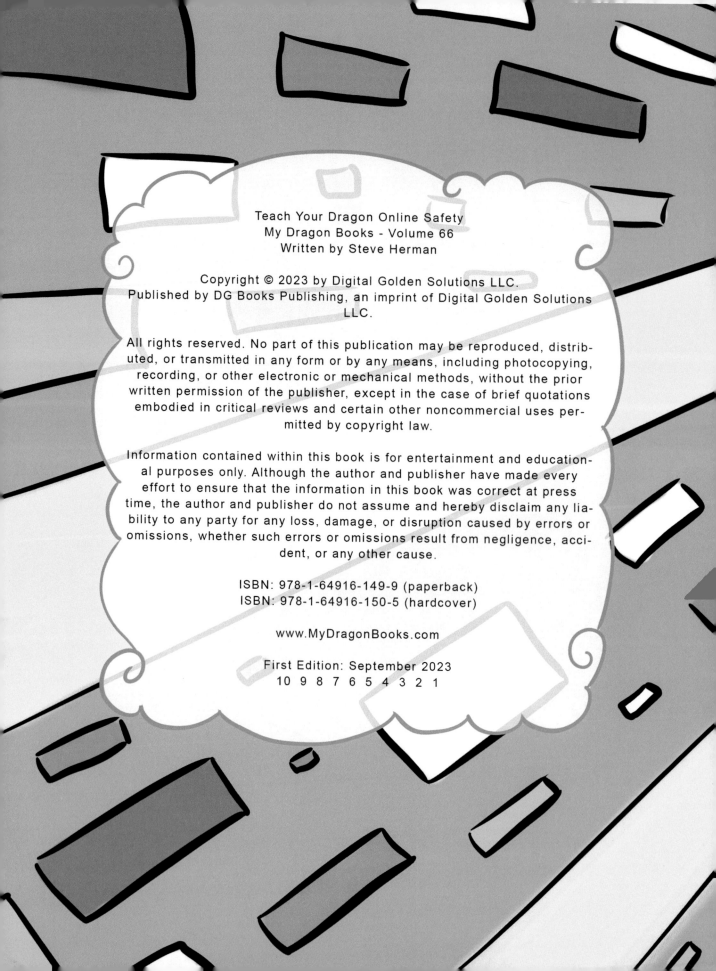

Teach Your Dragon Online Safety
My Dragon Books - Volume 66
Written by Steve Herman

ISBN: 978-1-64916-149-9 (paperback)
ISBN: 978-1-64916-150-5 (hardcover)

www.MyDragonBooks.com

First Edition: September 2023
10 9 8 7 6 5 4 3 2 1

Diggory's tablet and computer
really come in handy;
He uses them at school and for homework;
they are dandy.

He also has a phone that he uses
to stay in touch
With his family and friends,
for he loves them very much.

He loves games, videos, and social media –
Now, none of this is wrong,
But the time he spends online
seems to last a bit too long.

"That's not the only time," I said,
"you made a big mistake –
It could have been more serious
than keeping you awake."

"Diggory, as you played a game,
you began an online chat
With the other player."
Diggory asked, "What's wrong with that?"

I said, "Diggory Doo, a stranger asked you where you live; That sort of information is the type you must not give!"

Diggory said, "But he was friendly, and he thought we ought to meet. And then he said we could be friends, and making friends is neat!"

Diggory did remember; my dragon blushed and hung his head. "I clicked and bought those things by accident," he said.

"And what about your social media?"
I asked Diggory Doo.
"There are rules which must be followed
that I wish you knew."

"I like the way you share
all the cool things that you do,
Like when you baked my birthday cake,
and funny stories, too."

"But, Diggory Doo, not everything you post online is good. I have seen you post some things I don't believe you should."

"The internet is full of information
we can learn,
But *some* online content
is a cause for great concern."

"Some online stuff is meant for kids, but, Diggory, you will find Some are just for grown-ups. Please keep this fact in mind."

"Ask our parents or your teacher
if you ever are in doubt
About how to search the internet –
They will help you out."

"They may ask you where you live and ask to meet you face to face – But, Diggory Doo, beware! The internet can be a risky place."

"They may be *lying* when they say that they're a kid like you. They may ask for information, but don't give it, Diggory Doo!"

"There are questions you should ask yourself before you post online – Is my posting *necessary*, *positive*, and *kind*?"

"Will someone get their feelings hurt, or will it make them sad? Or will my post make someone smile and make their heart feel glad?"

"Don't tell someone online what you won't say to their face. Some things should not be posted in a public online space."

"That's right," I said,
"and something else I feel I should advise –
Spend less time on online games
and get some exercise."

Diggory said, "Let's start today!
Let's give our friends a call;
We'll invite them to play soccer!
I'll go get the ball!"

Diggory Doo was learning.
See, I told you he was smart
He listened to the rules,
and he learned them all by heart!

POTTY TRAIN YOUR DRAGON
Steve Herman

TRAIN YOUR ANGRY DRAGON
Steve Herman

THE MINDFUL DRAGON
Steve Herman

THE YOGA DRAGON
Steve Herman

DRAGON & THE BULLY
Steve Herman

HAPPY BIRTHDAY DRAGON
Steve Herman

TRAIN YOUR DRAGON TO ACCEPT NO
Steve Herman

I GOT THIS!
Steve Herman

TRAIN YOUR DRAGON TO BE KIND
Steve Herman

A DRAGON With His Mouth ON FIRE
Steve Herman

TRAIN YOUR DRAGON To Follow RULES
Steve Herman

TRAIN YOUR DRAGON To Be RESPONSIBLE
Steve Herman

TRAIN YOUR DRAGON To LOVE HIMSELF
Steve Herman

TRAIN YOUR DRAGON To Understand CONSEQUENCES
Steve Herman

TEACH YOUR DRAGON TO STOP LYING
Steve Herman

TEACH YOUR DRAGON TO MAKE FRIENDS
Steve Herman

TEACH YOUR DRAGON TO SHARE
Steve Herman

FIX YOUR DRAGON'S ATTITUDE
Steve Herman

GET YOUR DRAGON TO TRY NEW THINGS
Steve Herman

TEACH YOUR DRAGON TO FOLLOW INSTRUCTIONS
Steve Herman

A DRAGON CHRISTMAS
Steve Herman

HELP YOUR DRAGON DEAL WITH ANXIETY
Steve Herman

TEACH YOUR DRAGON MANNERS
Steve Herman

TEACH YOUR DRAGON EMPATHY
Steve Herman

TEACH YOUR DRAGON About DIVERSITY
Steve Herman

HELP YOUR DRAGON
Learn From **MISTAKES**
Steve Herman

HELP YOUR DRAGON
DEAL WITH **CHANGE**
Steve Herman

THE SAD DRAGON
A DRAGON BOOK ABOUT GRIEF AND LOSS
Steve Herman

DRAGON
SIBLING RIVALRY
Steve Herman

LIMIT YOUR DRAGON'S
SCREEN TIME
Steve Herman

DRAGON and HIS FRIEND
A Dragon Book About Autism
Steve Herman

TEACH YOUR DRAGON
GOOD **HYGIENE**
Steve Herman

TEACH YOUR DRAGON
ABOUT **STRANGER DANGER**
Steve Herman

HELP YOUR DRAGON
COPE WITH **TRAUMA**
Steve Herman

HELP YOUR DRAGON
OVERCOME **SEPARATION ANXIETY**
Steve Herman

TRAIN YOUR DRAGON
TO DO **HARD THINGS**
Steve Herman

TWO HOMES
FILLED WITH **LOVE**
Steve Herman

DRAGON'S MASK
Steve Herman

VIRTUAL LEARNING
DRAGON
Steve Herman

THE FOSTER
DRAGON
Steve Herman

A DRAGON
WITH **ADHD**
Steve Herman

GET YOUR DRAGON
TO EAT **HEALTHY FOOD**
Steve Herman

TEACH YOUR DRAGON
RESPECT
Steve Herman

TEACH YOUR DRAGON
BODY SAFETY
Steve Herman

THE BOSSY
DRAGON
Steve Herman

TEACH YOUR DRAGON
INTEGRITY
Steve Herman

BE A GOOD SPORT
DIGGORY DOO!
Steve Herman

A DRAGON
NEEDS HIS **SLEEP**
Steve Herman

A DRAGON
HAS TO **PERSEVERE**
Steve Herman

CELEBRATE
OUR **DIFFERENCES**
Steve Herman

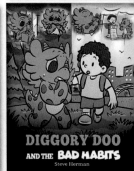

80226636R00031